The Snoopy Festival

Books by Charles M. Schulz

Peanuts
More Peanuts
Good Grief, More Peanuts!
Good Ol' Charlie Brown
Snoopy
You're Out of Your Mind, Charlie Brown!
But We Love You, Charlie Brown
Peanuts Revisited
Go Fly a Kite, Charlie Brown
Peanuts Every Sunday
It's a Dog's Life, Charlie Brown
You Can't Win, Charlie Brown
Snoopy, Come Home
You Can Do It, Charlie Brown
We're Right Behind You, Charlie Brown
As You Like It, Charlie Brown
Sunday's Fun Day, Charlie Brown
You Need Help, Charlie Brown
Snoopy and the Red Baron
The Unsinkable Charlie Brown
You'll Flip, Charlie Brown
You're Something Else, Charlie Brown
Peanuts Treasury
You're You, Charlie Brown
You've Had It, Charlie Brown
Snoopy and His Sopwith Camel
A Boy Named Charlie Brown
You're Out of Sight, Charlie Brown
Peanuts Classics
You've Come a Long Way, Charlie Brown
Snoopy and "It Was a Dark and Stormy Night"
"Ha Ha, Herman," Charlie Brown
The "Snoopy, Come Home," Movie Book
Snoopy's Grand Slam
Thompson Is in Trouble, Charlie Brown
You're the Guest of Honor, Charlie Brown
Win a Few, Lose a Few, Charlie Brown
The Snoopy Festival

The Snoopy Festival

Charles M. Schulz

with an Introduction by Charlie Brown

HODDER AND STOUGHTON
LONDON · SYDNEY · AUCKLAND · TORONTO

British Library Cataloguing in Publication Data
Schulz, Charles Monroe
    The Snoopy Festival.
    I. Title
    741.5'973   PN6728.P4

    ISBN 0–340–23315–X

Introduction

It is a great honor for me to be asked to write this introduction to Snoopy's book. Actually, I suppose I wouldn't have to do it if I didn't want to because, after all, he is my dog and I am his master, which means that he is supposed to do what I tell him and not vice versa. Sometimes, I think he doesn't know his place.

At any rate, this seems to be a pretty good collection of some of his latest adventures, but I feel I should point out that a few of the other kids around the neighborhood are here too. In other words, without them, where would he be? And as I have told him many times, without me, he'd be no place at all.

Anyway, I hope you enjoy his book. As Lucy once said, "He isn't much of a dog, but after all, who is?"

CHARLIE BROWN

I JUST SHOOK HANDS WITH THE EASTER BEAGLE, AND HE GAVE ME A COLORED EGG!

SMAK!

THE "EASTER BEAGLE"?

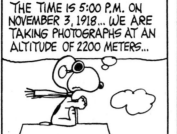

ON A WARM SUNNY DAY LIKE TODAY, IN A NEIGHBORHOOD SUCH AS OURS, IT IS NOT OFTEN THAT YOU'LL SEE A BEAGLE FLOATING DOWNSTREAM!

OKAY, WHAT SHALL WE READ TONIGHT .."TREASURE ISLAND"? "HANS BRINKER"?

"THE SIX BUNNY-WUNNIES AND THEIR PONY CART"... AGAIN ?!?

I DON'T UNDERSTAND WHY YOU WANT TO READ THE SAME BOOK EVERY NIGHT... OH, WELL ✻SIGH✻ "IT WAS A WARM SPRING DAY, AND THE SIX BUNNY-WUNNIES DECIDED TO GO ON A PICNIC..."

" 'I'LL FIX THE LUNCH,' SAID PAM BUNNY-WUNNIE.. 'I'LL HITCH UP OUR PONY,' SAID PETER BUNNY-WUNN...."

Z

Z

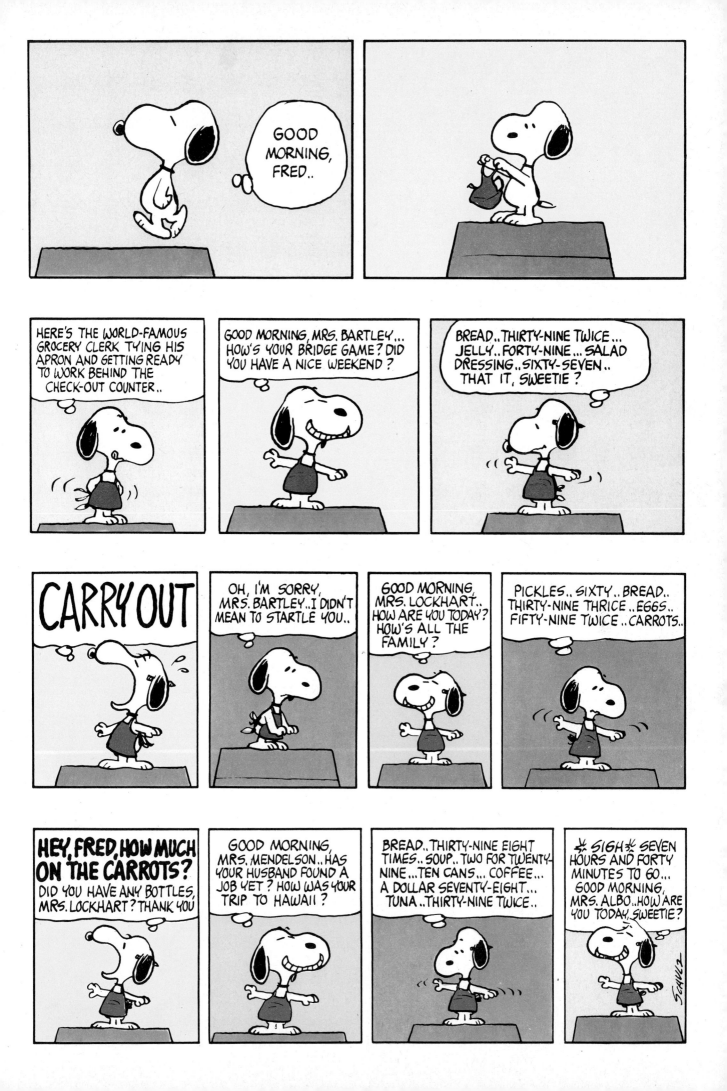

It was a dark and stormy night. Suddenly a shot rang out. A door slammed. The maid screamed.

Suddenly a pirate ship appeared on the horizon. While millions of people were starving, the king lived in luxury. Meanwhile, on a small farm in Kansas, a boy was growing up.
End of Part I

Part II.... A light snow was falling, and the little girl with the tattered shawl had not sold a violet all day.

At that very moment, a young intern at City Hospital was making an important discovery. The mysterious patient in Room 213 had finally awakened. She moaned softly.

Could it be that she was the sister of the boy in Kansas who loved the girl with the tattered shawl who was the daughter of the maid who had escaped from the pirates? The intern frowned.

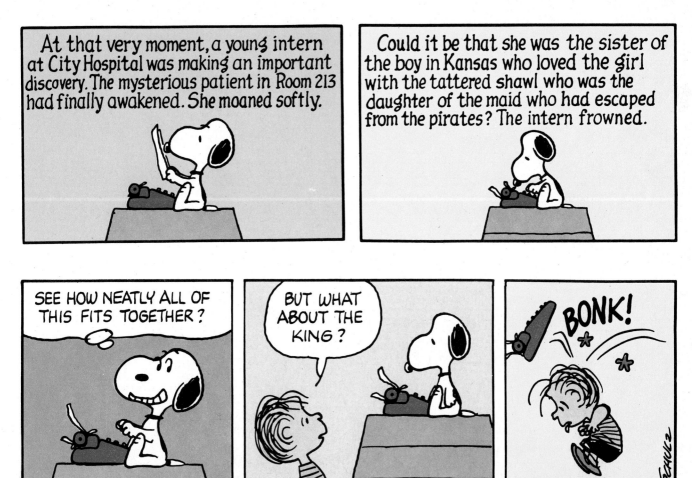

SEE HOW NEATLY ALL OF THIS FITS TOGETHER?

BUT WHAT ABOUT THE KING?

BONK!

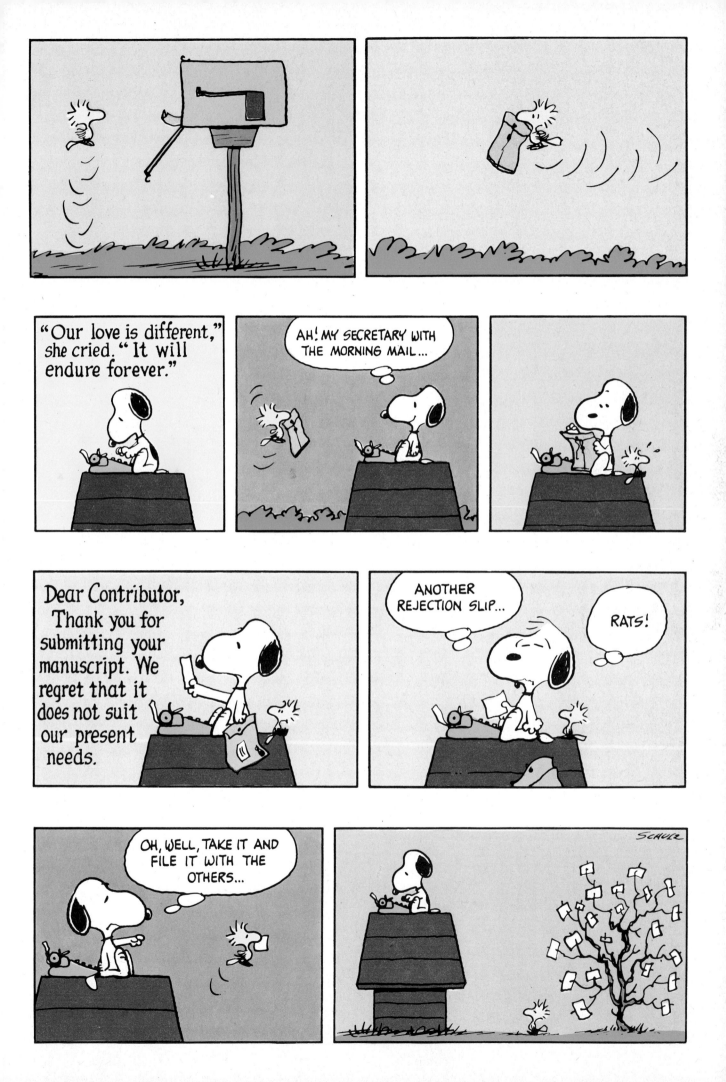

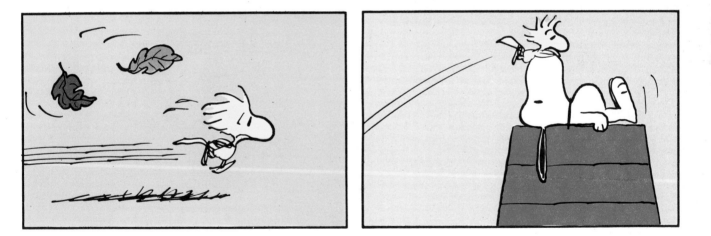

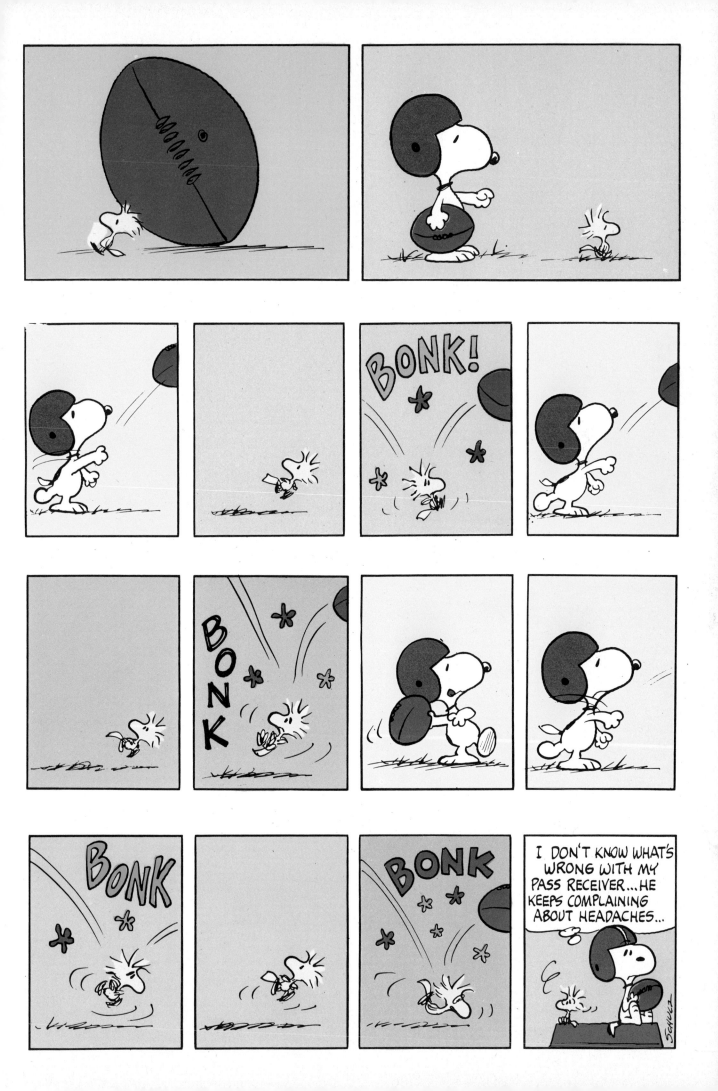